BECAUSE GOD SAID
"You Are Very Special"

BECAUSE GOD SAID
"You Are Very Special"

Karen L. Carlson
Illustrated by Sadie Clem

BECAUSE GOD SAID
"You Are Very Special"

© Karen L. Carlson 2013

This book is a work of fiction. Named locations are used fictitiously, and characters and incidents are the product of the author's imagination. Any resemblance to actual events or places or persons, living or dead, is entirely coincidental.

Published by
Lighthouse Christian Publishing
SAN 257-4330
5531 Dufferin Drive
Savage, Minnesota, 55378
United States of America

www.lighthousechristianpublishing.com

ACKNOWLEDGMENTS

I thank my Lord and Savior, Jesus Christ:

"Blessed is he whose help is the God of Jacob, whose hope is in the Lord his God, the Maker of heaven and earth, the sea, and everything in them—the Lord, who remains faithful forever." Psalm 146: 5 & 6

Pastor Jason Kelley, my son-in-law. BECAUSE GOD SAID was birthed out of your first sermon. Thank you, Jason.

I'm so thankful, Sadie Clem, that you agreed to take this book on and bring it to life with your amazing illustrations. We both stretched and grew throughout the process. It's been fun! Also, thank you Spencer and Jennifer Clem, for your encouragement and help.

Thank you Maya Lee, my sweet granddaughter, for naming " Froggy McButterpants".

DEDICATION

I dedicate, BECAUSE GOD SAID, to my precious grandchildren: Logan, Caleb, Jacob, Maya, Jonathan, Brooklyn and Joshua—the cutest and sweetest grandkids a grandma (AMA) could have.

My heart knows a deeper love because of each of you. I pray you will always walk close with Jesus and that each of you will make an eternal impact in God's Kingdom.

I love you so much!!! Jesus even loves you more!!!

In the beginning,
God created the heavens
and the earth,

God made you and shaped you before your birth.

Because God said,
"Let there be light,"

Because God said,
He made the sky blue,

He made the color of your skin and eyes too.

He knows when you sit and He knows when you stand.

Because God said,
there were vegetables,
fruit, and trees,

God loves you and everything you do, He sees.

Because God said,
He made the moon,
the stars, and the sun,

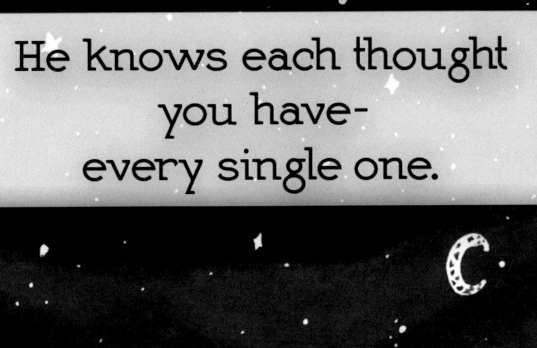

He knows each thought
you have-
every single one.

Because God said, He made the fish in the sea and the birds in the sky,

God cares when you are hurt and knows why you cry.

Because God said,
He made animals of
every kind,

Because God said,"Let us make man and woman to care for the earth,"

Because God said, you
are very special-
there's a one and only you,

He has a plan for your life and a task that only you can do.

Next time you go
outside, remember
to look and see,

ABOUT THE AUTHOR

Karen L. Carlson is married to her high school sweetheart, Terry. They have three married children and 7 grandchildren. Karen grew up and continues to live, in Stanwood, Washington, with her husband. She was the founder of MOPS (Mothers of Preschoolers) at Camano Chapel and was the first MOPS area coordinator in the Pacific Northwest. For five years, Karen, Terry and their three young children travelled throughout Washington and Oregon to help other churches catch the vision of MOPS. In 1997, they were the recipients of MOPS International's Heart of MOPS Award.

Karen continues to have a heart for MOPS and currently serves as mentor mom. She loves to share the truth of God's Word and to encourage all women, but moms with young children have a special place in her heart.

Karen and Terry started MUDDY WATER MINISTRIES to encourage and inspire people to glorify God, by using the gifts and talents He has given each of us to help others. To learn more about their ministry or to contact them, you can email them at muddywaterministries@hotmail.com or you can visit their website at:
http://muddywaterministries.tateauthor.com

Karen enjoys listening to Christian music, walking her dogs, going to garage sales, gardening, and having tea with friends. Her greatest joy of all is spending time with Terry, her family and her grandkids!!!

ABOUT THE ILLUSTRATOR

Sadie Clem has lived in the small town of Stanwood, Washington, her entire life! As of now she's coasting at the age of sweet sixteen, enjoying her sophomore year at Stanwood High School. Sadie lives with her mother, father and two brothers- and of course, the family pet- Lucy the dog. Her passions all revolve around words. This girl loves writing stories, reading stories- *sketching* stories, and most important- glorifying God.

Made in the USA
Middletown, DE
13 October 2020